This Storybook Belongs To

Princess _____

Cinderella

Once upon a time, in a faraway land, there lived a rich, widowed gentleman and his beautiful daughter, Cinderella. Cinderella's father was kind and loving. He married again so that his daughter had a mother to care for her.

Cinderella's Stepmother had two mean daughters named Anastasia and Drizella.

When Cinderella's father died, her Stepmother stopped pretending to like her. She was jealous of Cinderella's charm and beauty, so she forced the young girl to become a servant in her own home.

Cinderella was given a tiny room in the attic. There, her only friends, the mice and the birds, listened as she sang about her dreams of a life filled with happiness and love.

Not far away, in the royal palace, the King and the Grand Duke discussed the Prince.

"It's time he married," said the King. Suddenly, he had a royal idea. "We'll have a ball! And invite every young maiden in the kingdom. The Prince will surely fall in love with one of them."

The invitations went out that very day.

When the royal messenger delivered the invitation to Cinderella's house, Cinderella went to find her Stepmother.

"There's going to be a ball at the palace!" her Stepmother exclaimed, reading the invitation. "Every young maiden is to attend."

"Why, that means I can go, too," said Cinderella hopefully.

Anastasia and Drizella shrieked with laughter at the idea.

"Well," said Cinderella, "why not?"

Her Stepmother thought for a moment. "I see no reason why you can't go," she said slyly, "*if* you get all your work done."

"I'm sure I can!" cried Cinderella, rushing upstairs to find something to wear.

Cinderella opened her wardrobe and took out one of her mother's old gowns. "It's a little old-fashioned, but I'll fix that," she said.

"Cinderella!" shrieked her Stepmother.

"Coming!" called Cinderella.

Jaq, Gus, and the other mice knew that poor Cinderella would never have time to finish the dress. So, with the help of the birds, they decided to work on it themselves.

They used an old sash and beads that Anastasia and Drizella had thrown away for the trim.

Later that evening, Cinderella sadly returned to her room. She had so many chores to finish; there was no time to fix her dress. She looked out the window and saw the coach arriving that would be taking her Stepmother and stepsisters to the ball.

As Cinderella turned around, she suddenly saw the dress.

"Surprise!" her friends cried.

"Oh, it's wonderful!" Cinderella exclaimed. In no time at all, she had slipped the dress on and was running downstairs to the carriage.

But when Anastasia and Drizella saw Cinderella looking so beautiful, they were filled with jealousy.

"Why, you little thief!" Drizella cried, seeing her old beads. Then Anastasia noticed her sash. "That's mine!" she yelled, grabbing the sash and ripping Cinderella's dress.

Cinderella was so upset she ran outside to the garden and collapsed in tears. She did not notice the magical light swirling around her. When she looked up, there was an old woman sitting on the bench.

"I'm your Fairy Godmother," the lady said kindly. "Dry your tears. You can't go to the ball looking like that! Now, fetch me a pumpkin and hurry—even miracles take time!"

Minutes later, the Fairy Godmother waved her magic wand over the pumpkin. With some magical words, the pumpkin changed into a sparkling carriage.

"Now," the Fairy Godmother began, "with an elegant carriage like that, you simply have to have—mice!"

With that, she waved her wand over Gus, Jaq, and their friends and changed them into proud white horses. By the time she was through with the farmyard animals, there was a Coachman and a Footman, too!

Then, with a final wave of her wand, Cinderella was dressed in a beautiful ball gown and lovely glass slippers.

"Oh, thank you!" Cinderella cried, stepping into the carriage. "It's like a dream come true."

"I know, dear," the Fairy Godmother replied. "But remember, you only have until midnight. On the last stroke of twelve, the spell will be broken, and everything will return to the way it was before."

At the palace, Cinderella entered the glittering ballroom.

Glancing up, the Prince saw her and fell in love at first sight. He took Cinderella's hand and led her to the dance floor.

Dancing in the Prince's arms, Cinderella felt as if she was floating on air. Suddenly, she heard the clock chime.

"I must go!" Cinderella cried as she fled down the palace steps.
"Wait!" called the Prince.
But Cinderella didn't stop—not even when she lost one of her glass slippers on the steps. She stepped into the carriage and raced home.

As the last stroke of midnight was heard, the carriage turned back into a
pumpkin and Cinderella was wearing rags once more. But she still held one
glass slipper in her hand.

Back at the palace, the Prince declared that he would only marry the girl
whose foot fit the glass slipper he had found.

The next day, the Grand Duke began his search. Every maiden in the land would have to try on the glass slipper until the Prince's true love was found!

Meanwhile, Cinderella's Stepmother had become suspicious when she heard her stepdaughter humming the music from the ball. She was determined that Cinderella not try on the glass slipper. When Cinderella went upstairs to her room, her Stepmother followed her and locked the door.

At last the Grand Duke arrived at Cinderella's house. Anastasia and Drizella tried to squeeze their foot into the delicate slipper, but it was no use!

Jaq and Gus wanted to help their friend. They stole the attic key from the Stepmother's pocket and pushed it all the way up to Cinderella's room.

Just as the Grand Duke was about to leave, Cinderella appeared. "Please wait!" she called. "May I try on the slipper?"

The Grand Duke led Cinderella to a chair and called the Footman over. As the Footman stepped forward, the wicked Stepmother tripped him. The glass slipper flew through the air, fell, and shattered into a thousand tiny pieces.

Cinderella smiled and pulled the other glass slipper from her pocket. "Perhaps this would help...." she offered.

Her stepsisters shrieked as the delighted Duke saw that the slipper was a perfect fit.

Soon afterwards, Cinderella and the Prince were married. At last, Cinderella's dreams had finally come true.